He ... Me to The Feds

Natasha Neal

He Love Me to The Feds

~~ Acknowledgments~~

For

Bryce Adrian Mitchell

Because when you came into this world you taught me how to love and be loved. My sweet boy you will always be mommy's inspiration and motivation.

Ashley Blackmon

No words can express my gratitude. You pulled me out of a dark place with words of light and kindness I'm forever grateful. You're my person.

Sabina Lewis

Man If I could say thank you a million times I would. You are a beautiful soul and my true friend. Thank you for always fighting for me when I couldn't fight for myself.

Boss

Thanks for always being my confidant hot boy!

Mommy Daddy Tee and D Scruggs

Thanks for instilling love and kindness in me. Thanks for pouring into me. Thank you for being my village always!

Table of Contents

Chapter 1: On the Yard

"prison yards in correctional facilities."

I woke up and called my best friend Diamond. I asked, "Do you remember the guy from last night? He's been following me around campus for a while," I said.

"Keisha can you believe that he let you drive him home? What happened? Was he that drunk? Who is he? What's up with him? What you gone do?".

"Girl, so here's what happened"

It was 2007 right before Christmas break. I wasn't a big drinker and I didn't club much, but for some reason I wanted to go out. I got dressed in my head. I always created outfits and executed them from beginning to end, poses and all. I was a flat out, bad bitch. Dark skinned, big boobs little butt, and was super cool so all the guys gravitated towards me. I could work a room and speak to the hood niggas, and the doctors like no other.

Everyone would say, "You act like Kiesha from belly. Not ghetto Keisha from the hood.", and I was cool with that. This night, we went to a local hot club in downtown Huntsville. It was a Saturday, so we knew that it would be pretty packed. I wore a red dress and black heels. I knew I wanted to take a pic in the middle of the street. I felt super cute.

I had a curly weave and enjoyed my night. The club was getting ready to close and I didn't want to be in a crowd when we we're leaving because I drove.

I told my girls Diamond and Pooh, "Let's head out."

The club had a huge staircase. From upstairs, you could see everyone. We began to walk around. While walking, a guy grabbed my arm and said, "What's up I'm Cali."

He had on shades, gold teeth, and dreads. He wore jeans with dress shoes and a blazer, so I knew that I couldn't take him seriously. Yet for him to speak, was intriguing. I spoke with a simple hello and walked away. We got to the parking structure and the same guy was stumbling around searching for his keys. I said, "Hey Mr. Cali. Get in with us and I'll take you to your car."

He gets in my car and when he spots his car he says, "That's me."

I said, "The bright green charger?".

He said, "Yes." My homegirl then said, "Girl take him home. Matter of fact. Hey, Kiesha is gonna take you home," she told him. He said ok. I told them that they better follow me, and they did. I got into his bright green, hemi charger black leather seats, and zoomed off. This was where the rush started. This guy trusts me. He's drunk and I'm just driving, I thought to myself.

We talked and he told me that he was from Florida. I told him that I was from Detroit. I then asked, "Why would your name be Cali if you're from Florida?"

He laughed and said that he used to tell everyone he was from Cali, and it just stuck after that. He then said, "Give me your phone."

He began to go through my text messages. I didn't care, but it was awkward.

He said, "I want to take you out, but you gotta call and wake me up." By this time, we were pulling up at his apartment. I said cool got out to get into my car and go. The next day, I text him "Hey, this Kiesha from last night" nervously, not expecting a text or call back. Cali immediately responded and said, "Hey we can hook up after leaving church."

Church? So, this nigga drinks all night and goes to church? Ok whatever let's see where this goes. He had me come to his apartment he told me, "You drive because you did a good job last night."

We went to a local steakhouse and ate. We talked things out. He was cool, country and kind of mysterious. I had talked to local dope boys, so I didn't get that vibe. There was something else about him. He asked where I worked, and I told him Sprint. He then gave me his phone and said to change my number when I went to work tomorrow. I said "Huh?"

He said again to change my number because he didn't want anyone else interrupting us. He really changed his number for a fresh start with me? How lucky right… WRONG…

I changed his number, and of course I went through his phone. This would be the first and last time for a very long time. He had tons of chicks. Tons of convos, but the one that stood out was from his baby momma, Kobe. Kobe was begging him to do for the child and he was dogging her to the fullest. At that very moment I said, "No, not me."

That night I gave him his phone and he gave me a key. Can you believe that the very second day of us interacting, I got a key and alarm code? I was basically attached to him since then.

Our first weekend, we spent it out of town. He had never been to PF Chang. It was a place that was so small to me yet was so huge to him. I felt that I had one up on him. I took the nigga to PF Chang. While out of town, he stopped by a friend's place named, Black and collected money. He did it so casually, so again I wondered, "Does this nigga slang dope or what's up? Well I then found out. Cali gave me one hundred bucks thanked me for driving and asked what did I want to do next.

I said, "Well I want to know what's up with this trip, and who is the dude, Black? We were supposed to eat, and you are making stops."

He said, "I gamble I don't slang. Slanging bring you jail time and I'm not bout that life."

I asked "What do you bet on?".

He said "Anything."

I said, "Oh so if I win bets, what do I get?".

He asked "What you want?"

I said "Shoes, what about you?". He said shoes too. So that's when the bets began.

The next few weeks we dated, then time rolled around to Christmas. A weekend before we made a bet, it was something small. Maybe a game that I lost so I had to buy him two pair of shoes. When I went over to pay up. He had a necklace from Kays jewelers that I wanted. I sent it to him, not thinking that he would get it, but he did. This was the first of many guilt gifts. I don't know if he did it to be sweet, or to continue to set me up for the okie doke. It was a diamond pendant that I still have until this day. I don't know why, but I got it when there was an innocence in our relationship.

And like that circle it continued to turn and twist. During Christmas, he went to Florida and he purchased me perfume, shoes, and other things. It was so sweet. I said earlier that I wouldn't be like the baby momma. I naively purchased his little girl, Reese shoes for Christmas, not even knowing her but I did it.

Then came 2008. 2008 was when things took a turn. While dating, we talked about sex, but we both were timid in going through with it. I had only been with one guy, so I wasn't abreast of the tips and tricks that he would brag on. The first time that we had sex, I got pregnant. This really threw another level in the relationship. I cried so much that I couldn't see straight. It had been just a few months and I was pregnant? How?

That February, he flew us to Detroit for my birthday. He met my family and friends, and they all questioned his energy. I took up for Cali. I said, "Oh he's this… he's that…", but I really didn't know him myself. Hell, his name wasn't even Cali, it was Phillip. We returned and I felt stressed because the question was really on my mind. Who do I tell that I'm pregnant?

He told his mom, but I didn't tell anyone. This was the first of many times that I kept a secret, and no one knew but him. Big mistake. A few weeks later in March, my doctor called and said my levels were low and that I was in the process of having a miscarriage. Ten minutes later, I was fired from my job as a manager at sprint for a customer complaint of me closing the store early. As I drove to share the news with my boyfriend, the alarm company called saying that his apartment had been broken into.

He was in class and told them to contact me. All this in one day weighed heavy as I prayed hard and was answered. God said to take a flight. I then went on to Detroit just to clear my mind. As I landed, I got terrible pains in my side and started bleeding. I rushed to my mom's house. She told me to get ready for the dental appointment that she had made but she didn't know I was pregnant. During pregnancy, you can't take dental X-rays. I made an excuse of not feeling well and took a nap. I woke up to several missed calls and then my phone rang. It was my boyfriend Cali. He had been on the run for hours, then was booked for shooting into an occupied dwelling.

Chapter 2: Restitution

"When a court orders restitution, it orders the defendant to give up his/her gains to the claimant."

His apartment had gotten broken into several times. This time, a new maintenance man knocked unaware of the situation and break in. It was the day he was moving so he thought that it was set up and began shooting. As he told me what happened, I cramped like never before after hanging up. I went to the bathroom and three huge clear balls fell in the toilet. I felt relieved. I felt empty. I had just had a miscarriage, one of several to come. I returned to Huntsville and my boyfriend was released. It was now the start of a trial. One of many to come surprisingly.

What made me stay was everything was good when it was good, but when it was bad, it was bad. We began to grow distant. He began to lose everything he touched, and I just didn't want to leave him and be a casualty as well. I felt that I could help. I felt

I could push him. I felt that I was important. We prayed. We went to church and we did all that looked good. I thought it was right, but he was doing it for a different motive. After months of searching for lawyers, we found the best fit. He went into court and we stood in front of a judge. Something that could have been six to ten -years landed him with one year on house arrest and one year probation. We celebrated and we went to that same local steak house we had our first date. I treated everyone. The pastor, mother, friends, and family to dinner. I left early while they celebrated. It was something about that day that set the tone for the rest of the relationship. I knew that what he had done was wrong, but I made him to be the victim. I made it seem as if the system had saved him from his own self. I knew I should have left but the chaos brought us closer. After this we got more serious. We had never been too far apart, but we still had our own places. I spent more time at his than mine and I had a key, but he didn't. The gambling became more obvious. At this point, he got into purchasing chopped cars. A girl named Eboni, had introduced him to the game. She was a hot girl. She hung with all dudes, her ex had tons of money, and had left most of it to her when he caught a drug charge. He was serving twenty years. She pretty much stepped in as him and ran his empire. I had never met her face to face, but they spoke and hung out often. The nights that I couldn't contact him, he would be bowling or watching a game.

I learned his moves and he never changed them. Winter came around again and we both were extremely sick. We rushed to the emergency room as always. This time it was different, he was so dramatic. He used to have me take him to the ER for anything. He would literally get me out of bed because of a headache. He frequently got IV drips and we would be back the next day. He called it recharging, I called it a waste of time. He would bowl until he passed out. He would gamble and watch games all night. He would bet on anything that had a ticket.

This night we went to the ER and the doctor asked did he know anyone that was pregnant. He asked because like I said earlier, Cali came to the ER to get "recharged" often. We looked at each other and immediately said no. I took a test right in the ER and I was pregnant. This is when things changed. He expressed he had never been around when his first born was younger and wanted to experience that with me. I was unsure because I was on the fence about leaving, but I didn't want my child to be without a family. I told my father first, then my mom, then friends and other family. I was so happy but felt distance this time. He took a trip to Florida and spoke different. He met a woman who introduced him to taxes. They called her Big Hottie. Big Hottie was a nasty woman. She was always sick, she looked disgusting, but apparently, she was smart and had that bread. Everyone pulled from her. She was a Haitian woman who would put spells on anyone who owed her money. Nobody fucked with her. She walked around the hood comfortably in hundred dollar cars and dressed like she was homeless. Her glasses were huge, and she cooked her ass off. I never ate it. Her famous stew was a curry soup or something like that. It always smelled great but looked awful. Cali told me the ideas Big Hottie shared and I declined because I didn't think it made sense. But he went for it just as a here and there thing, but when it hit, it hit. I became very distant. I fell into the church heavy. I would leave pamphlets on his car about fatherhood and just stayed away. I spent my entire pregnancy praying for him. Our routine was dinner every Sunday and meals most nights, but we were very cold. I decided not to talk to him for a few months. He popped up at the appointment to find out the gender. I lied and said it was a girl because he was late, on the phone, and rude. That phone call ended quick. He cried and begged the doctor to check again. We laughed and said it was a boy. He begged me to go to breakfast after and I agreed.

While at breakfast he said, "Can I buy you a car for having a boy for me?"

"Whatever car you want," I said sure. He expressed how he always wanted a boy and knew that it was meant for us to be together because I was able to give him a little boy. He began to tell me how well taxes were going and that he would take care of whatever I wanted. But this time, he had been out of school and heavy into taxes and gambling. I was in my last year. We got back together during the process of getting me a car. I wanted a magnum and that's what I got, brand new, with no miles off the lot.

We were happy for a while, then the cheating started. Now ladies let's be honest. A woman knows who, what, where, and when her man cheats if she has anything for that man. Now if you don't care, you may not have a clue. I cared. I didn't love but I cared. The day that I got my car, Cali had a funky vibe. He had just begged me back, offered a car, and took me shopping. He told me how good his "tax business" was going and had a funky vibe so in true woman intuition fashion I waited. That night I got off of work, I called, and I said to bring my charger.

He said, "Ok. Once I get out. I'm headed bowling.

I said "Well bring baby girl over and then go."

He said no because she was gonna stay home with my cousin which is something we never agreed on when his daughter was in town. She always stayed with me. So, sign number one. Sign number two, he was getting out of the shower. We was on facetime so I questioned, if you're headed bowling why shower?

Sign three, he put on a collared shirt and sprayed Cologne... bingo time to bust him. I waited an hour. The longest hour of my life. I went to the two bowling alleys in town. There was no sign of him at either location. I went to his house. His truck was gone, and no one was at his house. Big mistake right. I then went to his favorite spot, red lobster. He was not there. Ok cool, one place left. What does he think is huge and is super small to me, but a basic country bitch would be impressed, because it's newly built and just hit the city? PF Chang. I pulled up in my brand-new magnum with a temporary tag on the window. It was freshly washed as I pulled in the parking lot and what do I see? A huge red Hummer parked right up front. His flashy ass was hiding in plain sight. I walked straight in work uniform on six month belly and all. He's not in the main dining area so I go to the bar. I walked right up to him and asked, "Is this a date?"

He rushed out and who does he leave? The church secretary Melissa that he's been cheating with. Keep her in mind, because she will come up later as well. I stormed out behind him while he's on the phone with my mother, explaining to her how I have him on cheaters. The nigga was looking for the cheaters van, and thought I really had him on the show.

I said "No dummy. I just know where you are at all times because you're simple."

He left the Melissa girl and then returned once he remembered. He took her home and started begging on my phone. This was when I knew he wasn't right. Here I am six months and said this couldn't turn for the better right? I wish I would have listened to my gut.

Chapter 3: Wolf Tickets

"False Promises"

The next day, he took me to our favorite place. We ate, I cursed him out, and he spoke on how scared he was. He bought me more gifts gave me more money and I stayed. This time he put thousands in my account. He said that he always wanted me to hold some of his money in case me or the baby needed anything. He then asked if he could get a fresh start. I agreed and just went along to get along. I became distant. I was processing him out. Shopping sprees, trips, and random gifts were daily. He asked for sex, but I declined. I knew of other women, but I didn't let it bother me. I wanted my child to be born into a happy place with no drama. I felt like if we were gonna be then it would be.

October 4th, 2009 we went to church, went to dinner, we walked around the mall and I stayed the night. The birth of my child began. These were the happiest times I've ever experienced. Oct 5th, 2009 Kash Meeks was born. His dad was so proud that he cried, laughed and he bragged. He then argued with me in the hospital about not having a biblical middle name or a middle name period. We were back to what seemed normal.

I had Kash on a Monday and completed my finals on Friday. I then graduated six months later and was really moving closer to what I wanted. He helped me so much while in school and working, because he was a great dad and support. I worried and wanted for nothing. He then asked to move into my townhome, and I agreed. We weren't together and we weren't having sex. I think he knew I was serious about focusing on our son and that's it. Memorial Day 2009, it was early. He asked for sex and I declined.

I said, "I'm not having sex Cali. Anyone that's not my husband can't get nothing from me. I can't continue to be a part of something that's not bigger than me."

With tears in my eyes I stood up and was proud.

He laughed and said, "Ok have a great day at work."

I came home and he had someone cook BBQ. I was making sides. He was on house arrest at the time, so he showed me a new Escalade from our front window. He said, "Eboni dropped that off today. Do you like it? We need more room with the baby, so I got that for us."

I paid it no mind because he worshiped the truck like he did all his other toys. Kash was asleep and he began to tell me how someone at church was engaged. I then began to dance and said, "I can't wait until my proposal I'm gonna dance for my husband."

He then went in his pocket, rolled over on the couch and said, "Show me your dances." I screamed so loud I woke the baby. He asked will I marry him. I wondered why my mom and friends were calling all day. I later found out earlier in May at my graduation he had planned on proposing while everyone was there. By him being on house arrest, things ran a little later than planned and he had to get home. I was elated that everything that had been done went out the window. I had forgotten all the disrespect and just enjoyed that day. He was so happy he smiled. He was proud, and we told everyone. A few were happy, a few seemed like confusion was their middle name, but I had gotten my man, my son and my degree this was good. We loved on each other from then on. He wanted a huge wedding I wanted to go to the courthouse he wanted fifteen groomsmen I wanted 1 bridesmaid, so we decided to get married in our church just he and I. We were heavy into church, so pastor Oliver was more excited than we were. Remember this man because he plays apart in the end as well. My family came his did not, not one person no one even congratulated us, but it was cool because we were gonna have our own family, right? We married in July.. by August we were beefing. We had gotten a house and I came home to that house one day and my stepdaughter was living with us. He paid Kobe $4,000 to take Reese and we never heard from her again. I didn't have an issue that she lived with us, I had an issue that we never talked about it. We were not even thirty days in, and another human is in our home with no room decor I felt bad I felt pressure I just wanted our picture to be perfect. Reese had a lot of issues at home with her mom she had several siblings and they were living in a one-bedroom apartment and sometimes in a non-working car. This was the beginning of our non-communication. I have major issues with people who don't communicate, and I don't communicate because each time I tried to voice or speak a thought I was shut down or ignored by my one person I leaned on which was him. Now with a baby and a kid I was juggling I had to learn how to cook constantly clean and just maintain a smile. Pressure grew tax money was running out for the year and he began to complain about me working too much. I was working my dream job I was happy I had a life outside of the home and he hated it. I had become such a housewife he tried forcing me to quit my day job. He would make excuses why he couldn't keep our son and force me to stay home. I started looking into real estate school he said if I pursued becoming an agent, he would pay for everything. Well this was the first time, well my fourth time trusting him blew up in my face. I would work then stay up all night studying and doing online exams. He started to notice my passion and stopped watching the baby. He would spend all my money in my account for the most random things. So how could I stop working finish real estate school and cater to the home? I couldn't do this. Me stopping and starting based off of his actions. At the time I didn't see what he was doing. He wanted me so dependent upon him that I would have to figure things out before falling on my face or go to him and beg. He then started to kidnap my son in his mini rants and episodes. How does a husband, father and man you live with kidnap your son you ask? Well when you pick a child up early from day care block the mother and stay gone all day ladies and gents that's kidnapping. Now it didn't seem that serious at first until it happened several more times throughout the relationship. He would block me and keep our son until he got what he wanted. It could be me cashing a check opening up an account anything just to make me do things. Let me rewind back to when I was pregnant, and we use to take trips often to Florida. We actually spent every thanksgiving of our relationship there. One time we were visiting he pulled up to a bank he said you have a business name established open an account and I'll make sure it always has money that way you are good. Now I'll say this statement again later and I've probably said it prior because he would always run this line. Everything he did benefited him. Him purchasing me a car he drove, us getting new houses he wanted that certain status, he wanted to be on a pedestal, I was just a trophy that it made sense. I had these things prior and I was the look he needed at the time. I began going to a stylist that was so bossy to me even her name was bossy. This lady real name was Peaches. Who has a name like that Peaches? She dated, she had nice things, no kids, just trips whips nice clothes shoes on point she did it all. So, I knew I could do it all. I also met my best friend Amanda who had been divorced and getting ready to have a baby so I knew it could be done I just had to figure out how. Arguments became more tense. He began to gamble, and I began to ask him to work. He gambled more and more. He stayed up and out later and later. I began to worry all while keeping up our look. During all of this we stayed in church we were armor bearers we did it all we hosted parties we paid for damages lights whatever was needed it was all like a game. Pastor Oliver and his wife Lucy would borrow our cars and money on a regular. They were at our home every weekend playing spades and telling all the church business. It was all a part of the game, and we didn't know when it would end. One night I asked his purpose I said you're my husband. I've taught you how to dress, I started an LLC for you, and you don't use any of the information. I've given you a son I raise your first child I cook I clean what do you feel you have to do. He looked me in my eyes and said nothing. He had never taken out trash prior to meeting me that was something his mother had done, and he was ok with just doing it for himself at his own home. He had never stayed in a house until we met, only apartments. He had never even paid a bill outside of utilities, so he felt more pressure than me. I was shocked how could I marry a man I didn't even know. And did he really even know me! But ok let me figure it out what do I do to make this look good.

Chapter 4: Crossed Out

"When a person is taken from a good area, job, etc. for something they claim not to have done, or for something that they don't feel they should have been blamed for, they say they were "crossed out.""

I began research on things he could invest in, each he would become bored with each he would give up on and gamble. So, was it me was I not enough or was he just lazy? I wanted a new house. Our family had grown, and I wanted more space. I adored Peaches and I loved her home even more. She was selling it and I wanted it, it was perfect. We looked, we agreed, and we sat down and gave her 20 thousand to move in. Peaches and I were cool, but we became closer after this. She had gotten married same time as me so we all would hang out of town. Her and I would go out and I really thought she was just schooling me on business. Plot twist, everyone is out for money and self-preservation. We moved into this home and

I immediately felt regret. He told me to maintain the home he just didn't feel comfortable with odd jobs and business and wanted something solid, he wanted to do taxes but this time on his own. Before I knew it, it made him happy but kept him busy, so I agreed as long as he came home by a certain time and didn't bring it to our home, I was good. Or at least I thought. We started having more company than ever more cell phones started popping up and the disrespect was just like we were roommates. He stayed on one side I stayed on another. Cars started rolling in more money accounts and then the verbal abuse. Now he had hit me before at the time he said it was a mistake and blamed me for yelling at him and trying to get me out of his face. He had given me a black eye and I said my glasses hit me and caused it. I didn't realize I was grooming myself to lie continuously for a man who showed me the truth by his actions. Being dismissed abused and talked about should have been enough but no I went back for more every time. I went back because the bigger the fight the bigger the gift. It became routine for me to ask for what I wanted and needed after being disrespected and abused the day before. It gets dark for a while prior to the new house prior to the ups and downs it was several moments of abuse that were ignored. It was good times but the bad covered them up. The new house seemed to have brought everything out every emotion resentment and thought. I was laughing one day, and he said why are your teeth not straight? You have cavities and when you laugh you can see them. Mind you when we met, he had dreads gold teeth and acne. Me introducing him to a dentist a barber and proactive changed that. When I asked about braces, he told me my smile was amazing and don't change it but now my laugh causes him to be disappointed in my cavities and crooked teeth. Weeks later I was getting dressed he came in the bathroom and said why is the bottom of your butt so black and when did your titties get that big you know you have stretch marks around your waste that's just nasty. I began to get dressed in the closet, we had separate closets with locking doors, so this became easy. I was no more than one hundred forty pounds, so I knew I wasn't fat, but the words made me seek surgery. I went to several consultations each one declining to do surgery because of the lack of fat to transfer each one said just go to the gym but

I couldn't go home and tell this man I'm going to the gym I wanted to have immediate results for him. It then was in my head I had to whiten my teeth lose weight work out dress a certain way do everything I thought he wanted. He would make me change my clothes before church and when we would arrive Melissa would have the same exact outfit I had changed just sloppily put together with cheap shoes and bad weave. During this process we worked out together he began to eat different and say well none of this matter because you're not light skin. I like light skin with long hair and that's not you. He told his wife this me his wife who he had chosen to marry and ask to have a baby by that blew me. I began to do what the fuck I wanted I cut my hair off I grew it back I gained weight I lost weight I was just so unhappy. I would come home early and fake sleep I would stay out to not talk to him we would block each other. I would be out of town and he wouldn't even know. I would stay at Amanda's house. He never called he never asked a question but every Sunday I had to get in the car with him to attend church he didn't even ask he would sometimes leave me. We were like ships passing in the night. We then got to a point of no sex and sleeping in separate rooms. He and I having sex was like a chore it would be so lazy and dissatisfying I would cry, and he wouldn't even notice. I would be so disgusted and sick to my stomach I would vomit after and he would just sleep. His smell made my entire body shake his touch made me quiver and I still smiled. I did any and everything to please him but if it had nothing to do with money he didn't care. This is the point where I knew nothing of what was going on with Cali, he and Eboni was doing taxes in hotels and I was living my life on my own. I had a feeling he had or was cheating, and I would always find out every time. One day in an off-tax season he spent money to do a club promotion. I felt something that night that woke me up later to find out he met an old chic Lana that he had cheated with before. That night they started talking again and he began something with her that was what he called head no bread.

Fast forward to August during our final separation before the divorce I saw all of him and Lana text messages and calls on an entirely different cell phone he had. I also found out he was selling weed out of her house and using my friends and people who worked and cleaned for us as mules. Everything was money everything was a bet or a gamble he would pay anyone for anything he never did anything on his own. I think back to during the dating process someone owed him money and he did dirt to them. One time he set someone's apartment on fire for two hundred bucks. Another guy robbed him. He had the guy set up and robbed but he never did it alone he always paid someone else. He always made himself invisible and at the end of our marriage I saw why. He always told me everything without telling me nothing he would give me an entire story and then just stop talking. It was a time I begged him to go to a family members funeral he said no I don't like funerals. I'm not going! While gone he said he's going to Ohio for one of his family funerals this was off because you just wouldn't go with me. Later I found out he was in Panama City on spring break. He said he didn't feel like asking me to go so he lied and went. Again the issue was communicating but of course when he came home, he bought me another car. Eboni dropped it off for him and I still had never seen her face. He knew he had done wrong and was already ready to cover it up. I went out of town another time for a break as I would always do. I came home to all our family photos being turned around and condoms in our trash. He claimed he used them to jack off, of course I wouldn't believe that, but I stayed for what I have no clue. While arguing about it I kicked the laptop off the bed and he then threw it at my head. It went through the wall and chipped our bed. We had several episodes like this, and I always just made an excuse. At this point I needed a way out. He told me he needed to do taxes for the year one more time and I could stay or go but he wasn't happy and prior to us being married he would receive oral sex every day and because he no longer could get what he wanted he wanted to make me miserable because he was. That was it, it may not have been much for someone to leave but it proved he didn't care what he said or did to me. We began to try and separate. He was doing taxes and, in the midst, took a trip to Africa. It was about seven o'clock in the morning in April of 2012 the FBI, the postal Marshall and dozens of agents were at my door with mask and ready to kick it in. His mom me his friend and Kash were home. I let them in not knowing a full investigation was under way and they had been watching our home for months. Several times I would say it's a guy with binoculars outside or someone is in our trash and he told me I was paranoid and had no worries, but he also was in Africa while I was sitting in our den worrying. They showed me pictures and I felt floored. I told them they made me think I was sleeping with the enemy. I denied it being Cali and knowing anything and I had a quick story saying I thought mailboxes and checks that were purchased and opened were from workers. So, when this comes up again let me be clear a lie is a lie and even when you tell the truth that original lie will hurt you. Ok they tagged and bagged our home they numbered and alphabetized everything they took my phone iPads and whatever else. But he wasn't there, and neither was his Laptop. My name was never on any paperwork just Phillip Meeks (Cali) and Eboni Rogers who is now deceased, so I didn't panic I didn't even worry. Rewind to when I said I've never met Eboni I knew she did chopped cars and had hella bread from her nigga, but this said tax evasion? When did they do taxes ohhhh right while they were chilling in the hotel she was providing names and socials for him as well. This was one cold bitch and brave too because later that night she knocked at my door and my mother in law saw her through the peep hole. That would be the first and last time I got a glimpse at her. When we spoke, we didn't speak on the incident. He waited until his return, took me to a park, and began to tell me that while in Africa he confessed everything he had done pertaining to taxes, gambling, and cheating to Pastor Oliver. After confessing he went to a local river, dumped his laptop, and prayed as if nothing happened. He then looked to me as we became partners in crime per say. He explained to not worry or say a word he said they had no evidence and I believed him. He told me Eboni had gotten caught up for some stuff she was doing for her man in jail and they probably just wanted to question him. But I saw pictures of him they came to our home. So, this didn't seem like just questions. The issues we had went to the side and we waited for this to come out. It didn't so I thought. Prior to this he had gone to jail a few more times. He was pulled over with tons of tax cards and money just random things, but I still stayed. Until he and his mother set me up and dogged me out. She threatened to kill me, and he didn't take up for me he laughed. I knew then once again I was done.

Chapter 5: Forfeiture

"the loss or giving up of something as a penalty for wrongdoing."

On one of those cold summer nights his phone rang at four o'clock in the morning. It was the same raggedy ass girl bitch Lana he cheated with several times, she was silent. I knew who it was without hearing a voice or seeing a name. I confronted him a woman will never have me down bad enough to question her over my man let alone husband. He pretended to be sleep and the next day jumped up took the kids and left. Now here comes another kidnap moment because I was angry and took his phone, his one of three phones, he kept our son until I agreed to return it. He blocked me of course and I drove where my intuition took me. Straight to the raggedy bitch Lana house. I knew she would be low enough to house him while he was in kidnap mode. Any other person with any sense would have let him do dirt on his own. I used somebody's code to get in her complex, parked and I knocked on her door. He immediately came out with Kash and

Reese. So now I have to get my kid back and humiliate myself again for this man. He drove me all the way to the other side of town where we lived. All I cared about was our son. His phone still in my pocket we talked for a bit and he stormed out. Mind you my car was at Lana's apartment I went for my son and my son only. So, as I sat with my son napping, I hear the power go out. As he left, he cut the power so here I am stuck no lights no car nothing just a phone full of text from February to August between him and her and whoever else. I sat impatiently, I couldn't call him because I was blocked and couldn't leave because I had no car and the garage wouldn't open with no power. He had locked the doors from the outside, so I had to open a window and get out. That's when it got low it got dark it got to where I knew not only did he not care about me but he also could care less about our child and what he was putting us through. I had a neighbor's phone that got me to a ride to get my car. I don't remember if we spoke or if he came home that night. I just remember that being one of many times where I said no more. Peaches began to tell me how he was trying to buy our home from underneath me and how he just would talk about me to her and her husband, so I began to get strong. I moved out I got a three bedroom apartment because he said we would work things out, he would help pay and eventually move in. That never happened I saw him out with other women several times and the women were of course friends or my so called friends. Lana even saw me out eating one time and I had ran into an ex she recorded me sent it to him and he blew up on me for nothing and I realized him and Lana never stopped talking and she was bold enough to try and spy on me. What she didn't realize is that ex she recorded me with saved her because I wanted to beat her ass for just because. He would leave women in the club once he saw me. He wouldn't answer my calls or pick up our son so when he saw me it was not only shame and embarrassment, but he knew I knew what was up. I knew he continued to lie he then didn't talk to me or our child for over seven months. He called crying asking to come back and I just didn't trust it. We spent Thanksgiving and Christmas of 2012 together and I thought maybe this is getting better and then new year came and Kash was sick. He came and got in the bed and started to vomit. I jumped up to clean him and care

for him. He walked out and said he couldn't
do this anymore and I haven't spoken to him
nor seen him the same since. We divorced
August of 2013 and that was it. One night in
September I woke up, packed a moving
truck and moved to Atlanta for almost a
year, he didn't even know I moved he never
called or checked. I saw him continuously
disrespect me and have no regard. He gave
me seven hundred dollars for my four carat
ring and we had moved on. I was in a very
dark place for a year and I then realized who
I was prior to him. I realized I created that
monster and knew I had to get out of that
space. I was over him, but something still
weighed heavy on me. Six months after the
divorce he was set to marry. Remember I
said remember the secretary Melissa from
church, well that's who he was set to marry.
Pastor Oliver announced their union and
would be the one conducting the ceremony.
Hilarious right. He began to tell me how he
called if off because she was extremely
jealous of me and mistreated our son several
times. He finally was being nice, a side I
hadn't seen since we first met in 2007. He
came around for a brief moment and that
was it. In 2016 I moved to Detroit. I began
to get my happy back, I dated I went out I

was myself again. In July 2016 I had to return to Huntsville for my best friend's wedding. At this point he and I didn't communicate. He rarely saw our son, but I knew we would be in town and I never want to be the mom that ruins her child's relationship with his dad, so I let him know we were coming. For some reason he was happy he was elated he asked if we needed money where we would be staying could we have lunch everything I was confused but went with it. Well as soon as we touched down, he needed me. He said he had gotten into a bad accident the car was at a local tow yard but it was in my name and he needed my ID for them to release it… now I don't know if you guys read that but he needed my ID to have his car released. I never even knew the fucking car was in my name how did he renew tags? How did he get insurance? A 2009 brand new at the time Escalade was in my name? The same Escalade he had gotten when we first had the baby. Now this is almost three years after the divorce in 2016 and you have a whole car in my name that you need me to get out? Oh no this was my chance this was my moment I'm gonna wait and get it out and ride back to Atlanta on his ass. What could he do? It's in my name, right? He dumb he shouldn't have told me that well that's not how that went. I did all the wedding activities rehearsal dinners the whole big thing. He waited outside of each event and I ignored him because I had my own plan. The day of the wedding he begged to get our son and I said he's in the wedding wait until after and he did just that. He picked him up at about nine o'clock that night. At 9:16 he texts and said if you don't get my car out of the tow yard your son won't be going back with you. Ladies and gentlemen another kidnapping. This may be funny to some, but this is serious, my son is all I have, and he knew that was the only way to make me move and/or hurt me and he did just that. I stayed up all night. I tried to facetime locate everything but of course he cut all communication. I begged him to return my son he said only if you meet me at the tow yard. He said I will give you your son and I will pay my back child support. So, like a dummy I agreed. Diamond and I went to the tow yard bags packed and ready to hit the road I didn't know what to expect I just knew I had to get my son. The gentleman at the yard asked was I ok and in any type of trouble. I made it look good and quickly replied no, my ex-husband is just meeting me here for our car. He sat in the car with my son until they drove the truck out and released it. The man again asked was I ok when he released the keys he released my son. After that we didn't see or speak to him for a year. I don't even know how he saw my son again for summers. I never want to tear down my son's hero but his cape had covered and destroyed me for years. I never communicated with him unless it was about our son, but something was still chasing me that I didn't understand. One day in January 2018 he called me on facetime. I didn't know why because we haven't spoken in years. My son went for summers and that was that. He didn't pay child support so what could he possibly want? He said "remember that stuff a long time ago? It's back." I immediately was in shock because why is he telling me I wasn't in the paperwork, him and Eboni was so what did he want me to do? A few days later he said Eboni was taken care of. At the time I didn't know what that meant and a few days later I found out Eboni was murdered while out to dinner with her new boyfriend, who called it in. Cali's best friend and his wife. Now this was strange to me. I immediately called Cali and I was in disbelief. He denied it, but in my heart of hearts I was unsure. I later was contacted by Cali's current girlfriend. She disclosed to me that he confessed everything to her how he had murdered Eboni and was planning on paying me off or setting me up to go to jail. He also had paid Peaches into saying she met me from doing her taxes and I would eventually force him into the life. Now I know that's all confusing because I'm still confused from the betrayal and lies. What no one knows is I recorded Cali's girlfriend at the time Nina because I knew she was a woman scorn and mad he had started cheating and beating her ass, but she later claimed everything she told me was a lie. No baby girl you just hurt and he's still able to manipulate you. But that's not my story to tell. We will let her tell that story another day.

Chapter 6: Hold Your Mud

"To resist informing or snitching even under threat of punishment or violence."

February 15th, 2018 at eight o'clock in the morning, the Marshalls were at my house to pick me up. I walked in and knew what it was for. What I didn't know was that this was the beginning of me finding out he had set me up. The probation officer looked at me and said this is your ex-husband correct, I said yes. I said but why am I involved she said Ms. Davis you know what you know but you never know what someone else says you know. Do not contact Mr. Meeks if you know what's best for you. That stuck with me. He called, he text, he reached out he sent money he paid child support all things he had never done before. He was nice he asked to buy me things he offered me two businesses of my own. Let me also say who did he pay to represent me? The same lawyer who had gotten him off on his first case when we first met. Lorenzo Swift someone I thought would save me but ended up hurting me more. Rewind to when I said that set the tone and maybe that's why.. The same exact man who hated my man then represented me now, but he paid him? Dumbest decision to date I've ever made. I wish I would have linked the feelings and discernment God gives because it would have saved me a lot but Remember the bigger the abuse disappointment or issue the bigger the gift. So maybe this twenty thousand dollar gift would buy me my freedom right? WRONG? We hadn't exchanged gifts in years so this one I didn't want. He tried to reach several family members and friends. He pretty much proposed for me to go to jail for him and I would be taken care of but why would I go to jail when he did the dirt? He paid for my lawyer flights everything and he said "You ok just don't say anything you trust me, right?" I looked at him and said Phillip I don't… No I don't." Everything changed from there. It was like we both knew what it was it was my life or his, it was me against him. All the abuse didn't break me all the lies didn't break me but for him to put our son in a position to lose his mom his only source of protection broke me down. I still can't wrap my mind around the hate he has for me. Months went by and to my surprise I wake up to a DM. Phillips girlfriend Destiny asked if I could call her and to not tell him or our son. I was hesitant, I felt it was staged but what could she possibly want with me? We had never spoken or met in the past and he barely even acknowledged her. I sent my number and to my surprise she called at five AM the very next day. She sounded angry she sounded confused and most of all scorn. She rambled on and on about his new girlfriend multiple kids she found out about cheating lies and how he was obsessed with me.. me? Now why would this successful man multi million dollar company having man who said I would never be anything without him be worried about me? She told me how he had set up Eboni and had planned on destroying me in court. He hadn't cared that we were married or had a child but in order to clear his name he would try and blemish mine. She told me step by step how he had blown up pictures and planned on presenting them to the court as evidence of a flashy lifestyle and bad mother figure. This was crazy because before he praised me as a mom and woman of standards. Now why would Destiny be calling me now? I didn't even know her name was Destiny until this very phone call. She cried she spilled her guts out but why? Welp I know why because he cheated. Hmmm now before she had no questions no words no nothing for me but here, we go he cheated while living with her and she now wants to know how I got from under the control of this narcissistic evil man. I told her to pray and believe in her own strength and that would lead her to better days. What Destiny didn't know was that I recorded each and every conversation we had. I had somewhat learned my lesson about this man and knew he could have paid her and from her conversation she was dumb enough to jump when he said jump. To cover me I recorded her. Her few weeks of desperation text and calls were irrelevant. I had bigger things to worry about. I fought the case for almost two years. I took a plea and didn't even know what a plea was. After all of that he stabbed me one final time. We were sentenced hours apart. The night before he wrote a sixteen page letter saying how I did taxes before meeting him and I forced him to do it how I set him and his family up how everything was in my name Wi-Fi, bank accounts, cars house everything. How I was this person that everyone loved and would do anything for how he never bribed or tried to pay me off everything was a conspiracy and lie against him.. . I work a regular job I live comfortably in my home I bother no one I pay taxes and do right by people this man has several successful shops tons of money has made millions and I forced him? I did taxes? I lied and threatened him to commit crime? Unbelievable right? Well in his eyes he's done nothing it's all me and has always been me. Now I'm a number in a system and have to serve twenty four months for a man who won't even talk to me for twenty four minutes without an issue. I have to hold my life and sons and families to do time for him. I was sentenced the end of September 2019 ten days before my sons tenth birthday. That hurt. I was honest, open and willing to do anything to make the picture perfect the whole time I was being cropped out. The end of October I did a radio show. Remember I said I had several secrets that I never shared with anyone but him well here's the last one. No one not even my mother knew the situation no one knew the times I was in and out of town I was in court no one knew the burden I was dealing with but me and Amanda. I always thought I would make it out I always thought my canvas would be clean I knew he would do me like this I knew in the end he would say it was him and my name would be clear. Eboni was dead so I knew it would all fall on him, right? Wrong. As we stood in that court room one room apart, he plead his innocence and vowed I was guilty. The pastor that once wed us stood in the gap for him and spoke on how much Cali did for the community and how he was this great guy. The same pastor Oliver who Cali has confessed all his wrong doing to while in Africa. The same pastor I cooked and entertained for. I listened in shock. They worshiped and praised him how he gave cars and material things and most of all cash. Cash rules everything around him but me. I could never heal before or after him because I kept pretending I wasn't hurt. So, what happened with me and the guy from last night that I dropped off? Girl I'm just now getting out the car I'll tell you when I wake up.

About the author

Just so we know what we're getting into. This book will have you mad sad and thinking about how and when to pick your person. Love is kind not complicated. Love is patient and not pressure. I've learned this the hard way.

I'm Natasha Monique Neal I'm 34 and my greatest achievement is my 10 year old son Bryce. I was abused for over 7 years but I'm no victim. I asked God to use me as a vessel and boom this book was birthed. I have an amazing support system I still love love and I know this is the beginning of my best days. This book is not intended to hurt nor harm damage nor bash or tarnish anyone's character or reputation. This is simply to expose the silent abuse I endured and how I survived. I pray I can help anyone in this same if not similar situation. We are here on this earth to give and this book is my gift for anyone willing to read it. I gotta do the calendar twice and that's a maybe so respect the game....

Made in the USA
Monee, IL
16 January 2020